AJ and the
COPY

By

Kimberly Waldren

Illustrated by Kaylah Walker

This is a work of fiction. Names, characters, places, and incidents are either products of the author's imagination or, if real, are used fictitiously.

ISBN 978-1-7379450-1-7
Published by Aleah Jean Publishing,
Glen Burnie, Maryland.
www.PublishedByAJ.com

Printed in the United States of America
First Printing, 2021

For my three daughters, Kaywa, Aba, and baby AJ.

Table of Contents

Chapter 1

Spots Suck

Have you ever had a day that just went from bad to worse? Well, let me tell you why Monday was one of the worst school days ever!

"Why in the world does your shirt have a bunch of huge pink spots all over it?" asked my best friend, Ashley Cruz.

"Well Kayla thought it was a great idea to wash all of the clothes at once. She's the worst at washing clothes and ruined my favorite Paris shirt," I said.

The shirt was a light blue, short-sleeved t-shirt with a picture of a black Eiffel Tower in the center, and the word *Paris* written in glittery purple letters underneath the tower.

Kayla is my big sister. She is fourteen, loves art, and is very creative with her work, but the girl cannot wash clothes at all.

"Bummer," Ashley said.

"Yeah, tell me about it," I replied.

After Ashley and I finished putting our jackets and backpacks away in our locker, we walked into our classroom to sit at our desks. I had always thought kids in high school were the only ones who had lockers, but nope, that was not the case. As a third grader at Cummings Elementary School, all first through fifth graders got lockers.

As I walked towards my desk, the third most annoying person in the entire world, David Willis, who had the blackest and spikiest hair ever created, blurted out, "A.J., you have huge pink spots on your shirt!" so the entire class could hear him.

All eyes were now on me and my spotted pink shirt. My classmates, Slime Ball Sam had the nerve to start laughing, and Stinky Breath Stacey started pointing at me and giggling too. I was so angry, that I am sure smoke was coming out of my ears. Doofus Head David, who couldn't keep his mouth shut, now had everyone looking at me. Before I could respond Ms. Wiley tapped her desk with her yardstick and said, “Okay class, clear your desks of everything except for one pencil. Pop quiz time.”

Every single kid groaned except for the second most annoying person in the entire world, Gina Wilson.

“Oh, yay. I really hope it’s a spelling test. Wait, no, a math test. I just love math so much. Please, can it be a math pop quiz Ms. Wiley?” Gina said as she tucked her long brown hair behind her ears.

Ms. Wiley stood and grabbed a stack of papers from her desk. She waddled like a duck as she handed each kid in the first row a smaller stack of papers so they could pass the rest behind them to the next kid.

“Yes!” Gina happily exclaimed. “Word problems are sooooo awesome.”

At this point, more smoke escaped my ears. Could the day get any worse?

Chapter 2
Queen Copycat

Finally. Lunchtime. I was officially starving. After this morning's pop quiz and group science project with Ashley and Stinky Breath Stacey, I had worked up a serious appetite.

Ashley and I walked down the brightly lit hallway and headed to the cafeteria. As we turned the corner, I could smell cheeseburgers grilling on the hot grills. YES! My day had just gotten better. Kids were chatting, laughing, and shuffling about inside the cafeteria. Ashley and I headed directly to the food line.

"How do you think you did on the pop quiz?" Ashley asked me as we stood in line waiting to get our food.

"Well, out of ten questions I'm sure nine of them weren't even from this planet. So, in other words not so great," I replied in a defeated tone.

"Bummer," Ashley sighed.

Our stomachs grumbled with hunger as we patiently waited for our turn at getting a nice, big, juicy cheeseburger and celery sticks with ranch. I always got strawberry milk with my lunch. It was so good and reminded me of a strawberry milkshake. I told Ms. Johnson, the cashier, my student number so I could buy lunch and then she looked at me and smiled. The big gap between her two front teeth always made me smile because it reminded me of SpongeBob SquarePants. She told me to have a lovely day and waved goodbye.

Ashley and I headed toward our usual lunch table in the far-right corner of the cafeteria. As we were walking, who did I notice sitting at our table? Only the most annoying person ever to walk the earth, Brooklyn Robinson.

I've known Brooklyn since the first grade, and for some weird reason ever since the beginning of third grade she has been copying everything I do, say, and wear. The crazy thing about it is that we are total opposites. I have two older sisters while she has two younger brothers. I have short and curly brown hair while she has long and straight blonde hair. I am one of the tallest third graders in the whole school and she's one of the shortest. I am the second fastest runner in all of third grade and she's the second to last slowest runner. And yet, she still likes to copy me.

Last week, my mom styled my hair into two curly puff balls. On Tuesday, Brooklyn came to school with her hair styled into two ponytails. I always wear my favorite Paris t-shirt on Mondays and Thursdays because those are the days I have P.E. Next thing I know Brooklyn had the exact same shirt and started to wear hers on Mondays and Thursdays too! My favorite color is blue so of course all of my shoes are blue. Sure enough, Brooklyn started wearing blue shoes to school too.

As Ashley and I walked over to the lunch table, Brooklyn started waving excitedly and motioned for me to sit right next to her.

"Hiiiieeee!" Brooklyn exclaimed. "Oh my gosh! I love what you did to your shirt! The pink spots really add a cool kind of style. Oh look! I got the cheeseburger and celery sticks today too. Maybe after school today we can play with Barbies at my house?"

"*Uhhh,* actually I can't. I have to *ummm*...I have to, *ummm*...study. Yeah, my mom makes me practice doing math for hours on school nights. So yeah, I can't come over."

Brooklyn's shoulders dropped. Her excitement quickly disappeared, and with disappointment in her voice she said, "Ok, well maybe another day."

"Yea, sure, maybe another day," I replied. Brooklyn's face then lit back up and her bright, big smile returned as she said, "Awesome! Oh, also my birthday is coming up real soon. Here's an invite to my party. It's going to be so much fun. My mom is ordering a huge blue cake. Half of it will be chocolate and the other half will be vanilla." Brooklyn then handed Ashley and me glittery blue invitations.

I glanced over at Ashley as she shrugged and bit down into her cheeseburger. With a mouth full of food, she said, "I love chocolate and vanilla cake. Count me there."

Great. Now I had a decision to make. Go to Queen Copycat Brooklyn's birthday party and be annoyed by all of her talking or come up with an excuse and avoid it all.

Chapter 3
A.J. Gets the Last Laugh

The rest of the afternoon at school went from bad to worst. I tripped and fell during recess while chasing after Fat Head Freddie who swiped my kickball as Ashley and I were playing. I also ripped a hole in my jeans and got mud all over my blue shoes.

At the end of the day, Ms. Wiley sent us home with math homework and a social studies project. The project instructions were to write about issues of the environment and how we could help make a difference. Then we had to create a poster that talked about it. Forget the environment. I had my own personal issues to figure out and deal with. My favorite shirt was ruined, my jeans were garbage, and my shoes looked like they had been through a war.

When I got off the school bus and walked into my front door, I heard my mom in the kitchen opening and closing cabinets.

"Hey! What's up, kiddo? How was school? Oh, my goodness! What happened to you?" My mom had finally noticed the hole in my jeans and my muddy shoes. I proceeded to tell her all about my day and how Brooklyn was sitting in my seat at lunch. She interrupted me. "Oh yeah, Brooklyn's mom texted me about Brooklyn's birthday party on Saturday. I told her you would be there."

Well, there you have it. I guess I would be going to Queen Copycat Brooklyn's party after all.

Just then, my second oldest sister, Ava, walked into the kitchen. This weirdo walked up and grabbed the kitchen counter with her right hand for balance, lifted her left leg up behind her back, and touched her toes to the back of her head. "I finally can do it mom."

My sister Ava is a level ten gymnast. Level ten is the highest level in the USA Gymnastics Junior Olympics. At thirteen years old, she is already being scouted for college. She really wants to go to UCLA and join their gymnastics team when she graduates high school. In May, she will be competing at the Junior Olympic National Championship all the way in Tacoma, Washington for the second time. That's a long way away from our home state of Maryland.

"Gross! What happened to you today? You look like you've been dragged across a muddy playground and then splattered with pink paint!" Ava disgustedly said.

"Shut up weirdo! Don't you have a balance beam you need to do a cartwheel on or something?" I spit back at her.

"As a matter of fact, I do. Ruby and her mom are outside waiting on me. I just came in here to grab a snack and now I am off to gymnastics practice. See you guys at dinner."

Ava ran off, grabbed her gym bag by the front door, and hopped in her friend Ruby's car to head off to practice.

My mom walked over to me, gave me a big hug, and kissed my forehead. She smelled like flowers with a hint of citrus fruit. My mom always smelled good, and her hugs were always warm and tight. The best feeling ever.

"Thanks mom. I needed that," I said.

"Hey, go ahead and clean yourself up a little bit while I fix you a snack. When you come back, finish telling me all about your day. I am sure you have some homework too, so go get yourself straight and hurry back," Mom said as she slowly let go of me.

After my snack and homework, I had some time to relax before dinner. I decided to call Ashley to come over for a little bit so we could think of new ideas for our YouTube channel.

Last summer Ashley and I created a YouTube channel called *The A.J. and Ashley Show*. So far, we have 172 followers, and we are working on growing that number. We like to post videos doing silly dances, pranking our sisters, conducting science experiments, and other fun stuff. Our parents help us with filming, but I think it is just an excuse to see what we plan to post.

"Hey, let's come up with a new prank," Ashley suggested.

"That's a great idea. Let's prank Kayla. Since she ruined my favorite shirt. It's payback time."

"Okay. That works for me. What should we do?" Ashley asked.

I tapped my chin with my pointer finger. "*Hmmm...* Oh, I got it! Kayla is always in the bathroom styling her hair in different ways. How 'bout we put some tape on the bottom of the faucet, then when she's done doing her hair and goes to wash her hands, water will squirt wildly all over the bathroom and especially all over Kayla and her hair."

Ashley's mouth spread into a huge smile. "Love it! Let's do that," she said with excitement.

We both scrambled downstairs to the kitchen. I searched through the junk drawer. Scissors, nope. Paper clips, nope. Pencil, nope. Stapler, nope. Pizza coupons, nope. Ah ha! Clear tape. We rushed back upstairs to the hallway bathroom that my sisters and I shared.

"The coast is clear," I said. "I'll put the tape on the faucet. You keep a lookout, okay?" Ashley nodded in agreement and then stood outside the bathroom door and looked back and forth and up and down the hallway to make sure no one was coming.

In just thirty seconds, I was out of the bathroom. We giggled all the way back to my room and waited.

About twenty-five minutes had passed, and Ashley and I were playing Barbies when suddenly we heard the absolute loudest screech ever.

Chapter 4
Dreadlocks, Back Flips and Butt Burps

It was six p.m., and the smell of garlic bread filled the air. I raced downstairs to see what else was for dinner, but before I reached the last step, I saw my dad walking through the front door.

"Daddy," I squealed and smiled so hard that my cheeks hurt.

"A.J., my bay-bey. Hi five."

My dad is my favorite person on this planet, right next to my mom. He is a graphic designer and an artist. He's very creative and a little quirky. That's where Kayla gets it from. See, graphic designers create movie posters, websites, and logos like the Target Bullseye, and other artistic and creative designs.

"What's for dinner sweet cheeks?" my dad asked my mom as he rubbed her shoulder and smiled.

"Today I fixed bowtie pasta with chicken and spinach in a creamy alfredo sauce. Oh, and a side of garlic bread," mom replied.

"Well, it smells and looks delicious," Dad said as he finger combed his hair out of his face. Being that my dad is artistic, he likes to express himself through his hair. He has dreadlocks which are also known as dreads or locs.

Dreadlocks are a hairstyle where your hair tangles and coils around itself into what looks like ropes or skinny twisted snakes. Not only does he have dreads, but his hair is cut into a Mohawk too! What's a Mohawk? It's a style where your head is shaved on both sides, leaving a strip of longer hair down the center of your head. It starts from the forehead to the back of your neck. My dad is very odd.

"A.J., help Ava set the table. Dinner is ready," Mom said as she handed my sister a stack of plates.

After the table was set, everyone took their usual seats. Kayla glared at me and tightened her lips. She was still upset with me because of the prank Ashley and I pulled on her earlier. I am sure she was thinking of pranks to do to get back at us. A few seconds later we said our grace and then we started eating.

"How was gymnastics practice Ava?" Mom asked.

"Mom, let me tell you. Today, I almost did The Biles," Ava cheerfully replied.

"What the heck is that?" I asked right before stuffing my face with garlic bread.

"It's a gymnastics move with a double back tuck and two full twists, all done when flipping off the balance beam. It was invented by the best gymnast ever, Simone Biles. She's the only one to ever do it, too, but I'll be the next," Ava explained.

"That's right Ava. Matter of fact, you should do a triple flip tuck cartwheel or whatever and throw up the peace sign as you land, then they'll name that one after you," Dad said.

"Dad, you're so crazy." Ava laughed.

"So, A.J., what present should we get Brooklyn for her birthday?" Mom asked, reminding me about the copy-catter's party, which I did not want to attend.

"*Uhhh...* I don't know. Kayla, you're pretty annoying like Brooklyn. What are things annoying people like as gifts?"

Kayla snarled, and before she could even respond, my mom jumped in and said, "Hey! Don't talk to your sister like that A.J."

Kayla glared at me and mouthed, "Sleep with one eye open tonight."

I rolled my eyes and said, "Fine. I guess a new Barbie and Barbie accessories. She is always asking me to come over and play Barbies. So yeah, something like that."

"Nice idea. We'll go out tomorrow after school, and you can help pick something out for her," my mom said.

As usual, Ava finished her dinner first. She eats food so fast like it will jump off her plate and run away or something. She ran off to do homework. Daddy finished his food up next, got up from the table, and started opening the kitchen cabinets to find storage containers for the leftover food.

Just as I was putting my dirty plate into the sink and turning to walk away, my mom said, “Kayla and A.J., since you guys are so in love with each other, you’re both are on dishes duty tonight.” I crossed my arms and pouted my bottom lip. I hated washing the dishes.

After the kitchen and dishes were all cleaned up, Mom checked my homework. I had already taken my shower for the night. I had even selected my outfit for school the next day. I decided to wear blue jeans and my purple and blue, flip sequined, mermaid t-shirt. As I climbed into my bed and pulled my blankets up, Dad knocked on my bed-room door and walked into my room.

"Hey there. All ready for school tomorrow?" He asked.

"Yep. Got my outfit ready, and my homework is packed away in my backpack," I responded.

"Good girl." My dad took a seat on the edge of my bed and patted my legs. "Look, I wanted to chat with you really quick about something." He put on his serious but concerned and caring face.

"What's up?" I asked.

"Well, earlier at dinner you said Brooklyn was annoying. Why do feel that way?" he asked.

I was a little shy about opening up my feelings, but my dad was easy to talk to, so I took a deep breath and said, "Well, she's just always copying everything I do. She tries so hard to dress like me, talk like me, and even tries to wear her hair like mine. Oh, and she talks soooo much. It's just really annoying Daddy."

My dad took a second to think and then said, "Well, why do you think she tries to copy you and talks a lot?"

"I don't know. Maybe because she just loves to be annoying. There are people who just go around bugging other people all the time just like mosquitos."

"I'm sure Brooklyn doesn't want to be annoying just for the sake of being annoying. Sometimes there are deeper and more specific reasons behind why people act the way they do. Have you ever talked to her about it?"

"No," I replied.

"Do you ever notice her talking or playing with anyone else?" Dad asked.

"Nope," I replied.

He then asked, "Have you ever noticed her copying anyone else?"

"Nope," I responded again.

"Does she normally go around smiling and chatting all the time or just around you?" he asked.

"I haven't ever really noticed honestly," I said.

My dad then said, "As the week goes on, starting tomorrow, I want you to pay attention to Brooklyn a little more. Tell me some things you notice about her moods and her interaction with others. Maybe we can figure out why she likes to copy you and not others so much. And please, be a little nicer to her and actually take some time to talk to her and get to know her. You never know how being nice to people can help their entire world light up."

Thinking about what he said, I replied, "Okay, Daddy. I will work on being nicer to Brooklyn, and I'll look to see if maybe there's a reason why she's always copying me. As weird as it may be, and as much as it annoys me, maybe she does have a good reason for it."

Dad leaned over, kissed my forehead, and gave me a big hug. "That's my girl. Love you."

"Love you too Daddy," I softly replied.

Then he walked toward my bedroom door to leave. As he grabbed the doorknob with his left hand and reached to turn off my light switch with his right hand, he looked over his right shoulder back at me and said, "One more thing."

"Yes Daddy?" I asked with a curious look.

"Here's something to remember me by."

He let out a loud and strong fart like a trombone doing a solo concert. It was the worst butt burp ever!

"Seriously? That was so gross Dad," I said with a disgusted look on my face.

He laughed, cut the light switch off, and walked out of my room.

Chapter 5

A.J. the Private Detective

On Tuesday, I woke up feeling pretty good about the day. As I ate my Frootie Tootie cereal, I decided I would work on gathering clues about Brooklyn like a detective or spy. I would lurk around the school hallways while spying on Brooklyn at a safe and hidden distance. I planned to interview her, but in a chill way, so I wouldn't tip her off as to why I was questioning her.

My bus stop was the first stop on the bus route. At exactly 8:25 A.M., bus number 136 stopped at the corner of my street. The big yellow doors opened, and I grabbed the handrail and climbed up the steps. I then greeted the bus driver. "Hi, Ms. Wanda."

"Good morning, A.J. Love your mermaid sequined shirt," Ms. Wanda said.

"Thank you," I replied with a smile on my face.

I decided to head to the back of the bus. I never sat in the back, but this day I had to keep a low profile. The next stop is where Ashley got on. Ashley was the third kid to board the bus. I saw her walking down the middle of the aisle looking to the left and then to the right. She was looking for me. I waved my hand and motioned for her to come sit in the back with me.

"Hey. Happy Tuesday," Ashley said in a cheerful voice. "Why are you sitting all the way back here?"

"I need to keep a low profile," I whispered as I scooted down in my seat.

"For what?" Ashley whispered back as she scooted down in the seat too. "And why are we whispering?"

I then told Ashley that I was on a mission to figure out Brooklyn's deal with me. I told her I planned to start off with a little spying to watch Brooklyn's daily actions.

"I have to keep a low profile, so she doesn't know I'm spying on her. Then probably during recess, I'll interview her. But not like with a microphone in her face. She'll get suspicious then. I'll just, you know, calmly talk to her and ask her some not-so-random-but-random questions."

"*Ooooh.* This sounds like fun. Can I be on your detective or spy team too?" Ashley asked.

"I thought you'd never ask. We'll call ourselves The Double Detectives," I excitedly replied.

"I love it," Ashley squealed.

"*Shhh!* Keep it down. You'll blow our cover," I said.

The fourth stop was Brooklyn's. By now the bus had gotten full. Brooklyn got on the bus wearing a blue shirt that had the phrase *Girls Rule!* on it and a pair of blue jeans. She started walking toward the back of the bus looking to her left and her right. Jeremy, a fourth grader with the brightest, most orangest red hair blurted out, "Keep it walking, short stuff. This seat is taken."

Brooklyn then reached the middle of the bus and stopped next to Natasha, a sassy third grader who carried a purse that held her lip gloss and cell phone in it.

"Seriously? *Ugghhh*... I swear, you better not touch me, or I'll push you down right on to the floor," Natasha said.

Two girls, Ebony and Crystal, also third graders, sitting right behind her, giggled. Brooklyn sat down, squeezed her backpack in her lap, held her head down, and said nothing.

After one more stop and a ten-minute ride, the bus pulled to the front of the school, and everyone stood and started crowding in the aisle. Since I was sitting so far in the back of the bus, it seemed to take forever before I finally got off. I looked around to see if I saw Brooklyn, and nope. Ashley and I made our way off the bus. We then entered the school and walked upstairs to the second floor and to our lockers, slightly forgetting about our mission of spying on Brooklyn.

"Hiiieeee! What's up, A.J.? Think you can come over and play Barbies today? Oh wait, you said not during the school week. I guess that's fine since I'll be seeing you Saturday for my birthday party. Oh boy, I can't wait until

Saturday. I really hope you like my cake. Did I tell you it's blue?" Brooklyn rambled.

"Brooklyn! Girl, calm down. Geez. You're going extra crazy right now," I said with my nose wrinkled up, puckered lips, and eyebrows slanted.

Brooklyn's smile and excitement quickly vanished like free candy does on Halloween.

"I mean, I know you're excited and all, but take a chill pill," I said.

Brooklyn looked up at me again and said, "Sorry. I'm just so excited about this weekend."

"I get it. But *ummm,* let's hurry and get into the classroom before Ms. Wiley comes out here bugging us," I said.

Brooklyn smiled and turned to walk into the classroom, but suddenly stopped and turned back around towards me.

"Thank you for always being so nice to me, A.J. You're the best," Brooklyn said with the biggest smile I'd ever seen. I'm sure I saw every single tooth she had in her mouth.

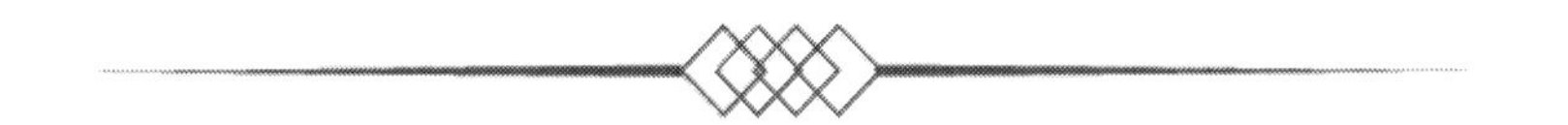

The day proceeded as normal. Morning announcements, guided reading time, math problem solving drills, media center visit, and then lunch. As Ashley and I headed to the cafeteria I asked her, "So, what do you think are some good questions to ask Brooklyn? I have a few, but I'm not sure if I should add more."

Ashley thought for a second and then said, "*Hmmm*... Oh, ask her what she'd like for her birthday, and maybe ask her what she plans to wish for on her birthday."

I replied, "Wow, those are really good questions. I think I'm going to also ask her what her favorite subject is in school, what she likes most about school, and I will ask her if she could change anything at school, what would it be. When she answers these questions, I will be able to understand her life better and why she's the way she is. You mind secretly taking notes while I ask the questions?"

"Good idea. And sure thing. I have my mini notepad and pen in my back pocket," Ashley said.

"*Mmmm*... You smell that?"

Ashley and I locked eyes and blurted out, "Taco Tuesday!"

After going through the food line, we made our way to our normal lunch table. Both of us had soft taco shells, seasoned ground beef, and shredded cheese on our lunch trays. I had my typical strawberry milk, and Ashley decided on chocolate milk.

Brooklyn was again seated at our table.

"Hi, guys. Oooh, they had tacos? If I had known that I would not have brought my lunch today. Oh well," Brooklyn said.

Ashley and I sat down. I glanced over at Ashley, and she nodded, suggesting I should go ahead and begin my questioning.

"So, Brooklyn, what types of presents are you hoping to get?" I asked as cool as possible.

Brooklyn's eyes lit up, and she smiled so big. "Oh my gosh, I've been telling my mom about the new Totally Hair Barbie Doll, the one that grows the really long and colorful ponytail! I want that one sooo bad," Brooklyn cheerfully responded.

"Wow, yeah, I know exactly which one you're talking about. You'd be the coolest girl in all of third grade if you got that Barbie."

Brooklyn looked down at her lap shyly. "You think so A.J.?" she asked with uncertainty.

"No doubt. I don't think even Natasha has that Barbie," I replied with confidence.

Brooklyn looked up at me and smiled.

"What about your birthday wish? Know what you're going to wish for yet?" I asked.

"Yep. I've been thinking about it for three whole weeks now," Brooklyn said.

"Well, whatcha gonna wish for?" I asked.

I saw Ashley out of the corner of my eye ready to take notes in her lap.

"Nope. I'm not gonna tell. If I do, then it won't come true silly," Brooklyn replied, still smiling.

"Oh yeah, you're right. I forgot about that." I then took a huge bite out of my greasy taco. *Mmmm*... Tacos are so good.

Ashley then chimed in and said, “I’m so glad it’s Tuesday because today we have art class after recess. I love art class so much. It’s my favorite subject. What’s your favorite subject Brooklyn?” Ashley looked at me and winked her right eye. She’s an awesome partner. She slid in a random-but-not-so-random question on her own.

“My favorite subject in school is reading,” Brooklyn stated. “Whenever I read books, it’s like I’m inside of another world. I get to travel to places I’ve never been, meet new and exciting people, and live out new adventures. I also get to escape the bullies around me. When I read a book, it’s almost like I disappear. I just love everything about reading.”

“Wow. I’ve never heard someone describe reading a book and make it sound so interesting,” I said.

We continued to eat our lunches and talk about some of our most favorite books. We barely heard the lunch bell ring because we were talking and laughing about books. We cleaned our table and headed to the trash bins to throw away our trash.

"Hey Brooklyn, do you want to hang with us at recess?" I asked as the three of us headed through the exit door of the cafeteria.

Brooklyn's eyes lit up with excitement. "Well, I was going to go to the media center and read, but ABSO-FREAKING-LUTELY! I would love to play with you guys at recess!" Brooklyn shouted.

"Awesome. One of our favorite things to do is walk the soccer field and come up with ideas for our YouTube channel. Maybe we can have you as a special guest on *The A.J. and Ashley Show,*" Ashley said.

"Sounds fun," Brooklyn replied.

As we stepped foot outside, the warm spring air greeted our faces with a golden smile. So naturally, we smiled back. A monarch butterfly with its reddish-orange wings outlined in black, fluttered by me as we headed toward the soccer field. The three of us started our walk around the field.

"Okay, let's practice our interview questions with you Brooklyn." I then asked, "If you could change anything in the whole wide world, what would it be?"

Brooklyn thought for a second. "Well, if I could change anything at our school, and only one thing, there would be no more bullies, or no more picking on others ever again. I hate it when people laugh at me for no real reason. I'm not really good with fashion or picking out popular styles. I'm not very fast so no one ever picks me to be on their teams. I like to read books instead of playing on cell phones, so that means no one thinks I'm cool. The kids always laugh and make fun of me. The world would be so much better if people didn't bully and make fun of others. Only if everyone was as nice as you A.J.," Brooklyn said.

Because I never took the time to talk to Brooklyn and really pay attention to her, I had no idea she was being picked on.

"Because no one ever picks on you like they do me, I thought it would be a good idea to start copying some of your style. And because you're always so nice to me I started trying to be around you more often. You make me smile A.J.," Brooklyn said with a smile.

Wow. I didn't know Brooklyn was going through so much. It wasn't until today on the bus I had ever seen some-one act mean towards her.

"Brooklyn, I'm sorry you've been dealing with all of that," I said.

"Yeah, me too. Sorry to hear about all of the bullying you've dealt with," Ashley replied.

"Thanks. I really think you two are the nicest people in this entire school," Brooklyn said with a big smile.

"Come on. Let's hug it out," Ashley said.

We all stopped and had a big group hug.

"Brooklyn, we got your back girl. I promise to pay more attention and stick up for you when I see someone picking on you," I swore to Brooklyn.

"Me too," Ashley chimed in.

Just then, we heard the loud whistle of Mr. Anderson, one of the third-grade teachers. Recess was over. As we walked back to class, I was no longer in my double detective mode. I was now A.J., the Anti-Bully Agent.

Chapter 6
Flava in Ya Ear

Tuesday evening's dinner was amazing. My mom fixed fish tacos. Boy, do I love Taco Tuesdays.

"How was school today girls?" Mom asked.

"Awesome sauce. We finally started to dissect our earthworms during science class today," Kayla spoke up.

"Super cool Kayla," my dad said.

"Yuck! Worms are gross, and the fact that you're cutting into one is even grosser," Ava said.

"Yeah, I'd have to agree with Ava on this one. That sounds gross," I said.

My mom chimed in and said, "Well, as long as it's educational and you're learning something valuable, I think it's super cool too, and yet, also super gross. So, let's change the subject at the dinner table, please."

I spoke up and said, “Today during lunch and recess, I got to talk to and learn more about Brooklyn like you suggested Daddy. She told me and Ashley she’s being bullied.” Everyone at the dinner table gasped.

“Yeah, pretty messed up right? Ashley and I told her we got her back and from now on we’ll be sure to speak up if or when we see someone picking on her.”

“Good girl A.J.,” Mom said. “If you ever see other kids getting picked on, it’s always the right thing to speak up for them and tell a grown-up. It’s never okay to bully someone or stand by and let someone else get bullied. Use your voice to help others and do what’s right.”

Then my dad said, “Like I always say, *treat others the way you want to be treated.* We’re very proud of you for recognizing that Brooklyn was being treated unkindly and stepped up to be her supporter and someone she can rely on to be her friend. That’s what true friendship is all about.”

My mom's and dad's comments really made me feel good. It felt good to know I was doing something good.

"Yeah, yeah, yeah. Enough of all that mushy stuff. Let me tell you what happened today in art class," Ava said. Ava is so animated when she tells a story. This girl literally stood up from the table to act out what happened.

"So, during art class, the kids were being all loud and extra talkative. No one was paying attention to our art teacher, Mr. Minton, or anything he was saying. He was trying his best to get all the kids to quiet down but had no luck."

Ava climbed up and stood on top of the dining room chair she was sitting in, then said, "Then, out of nowhere, Mr. Minton climbed on top of the large wooden art table in the middle of the classroom and blurted out rapping.

He was like, "I'm kicking new *flava* in your ear. Mack's a brand-new *flava* in ya ear."

And before Ava could finish, both my mom and dad joined in and start rapping along!

"Here comes the brand-new *flava* in ya ear," they said in unison.

"Oh snap. That was the jam back in the day," Mom called out.

"And the remix with The Notorious B.I.G., L.L. Cool J, and Busta Rhymes is such a classic," Dad added.

Ava, Kayla, and I looked back and forth between our parents with our lips curled up and our eyes squinted.

"Oh, oh, sorry. Finish your story Ava," Mom said with a slight chuckle and smile.

"*Ummm...* yeah, so long story short, all the kids in the class stopped doing whatever they were doing and looked at Mr. Minton the same way we just looked at you two weirdos." "Yeah, you guys are weirdos. Why would anyone kick seasonings into someone's ears?" I asked.

Both of my parents threw their heads back and let out the loudest laugh I had ever heard. I promise they laughed for a full five minutes. My dad was laughing so hard he grabbed his chest as he tried to catch his breath.

"What in the world is so funny?" I asked.

As my dad tried to catch his breath, he said, "It's Not. Seasoning!" And then he laughed even more.

I turned to look at my mom. She was still laughing, and tears had started falling from her eyes. I frowned.

"What's so funny?" I raised my voice a little louder. I looked over at my sisters, and they both shrugged.

My mom picked up a napkin from the table and wiped her eyes. She then said, "The song isn't talking about seasonings, honey. *Flava* is referring to the good sounds the rappers are giving to the listeners through their rhymes."

After a few more laughs and my dad finally catching his breath, both of my parents let out a deep sigh.

"Oh, my goodness. I needed that laugh," Mom stated.

"Yeah A.J., you really crack me up sometimes. That was a good one," Dad added.

"Whatever. You guys are just as strange as Mr. Minton, obviously. That rap sounds so lame," I replied.

Kayla chimed in and said, "Speaking of flava, can someone pass me another piece of fish please? These tacos are kicking *flava* in my mouth."

Laughter exploded from everyone around the dinner table.

Chapter 7

Want Me to Spill the Beans?

The next morning, I woke up a little more tired than usual. That's because after dinner, my family and I decided to play Monopoly. It was so much fun but staying up an extra forty-five minutes really had me feeling tired in the morning, yet I was in a good mood. Mom and Dad telling me how proud they were of me for my readiness to stand up against bullying yesterday had me feeling good about my-self.

The morning went on as usual. Gina Wilson was being her typical teacher's pet self and begging for another pop quiz. Luckily, Ms. Wiley didn't give us one. Stinky Breath Stacey kept leaning over and asking me if she could copy all of my worksheets. Her breath kept making my eyes water.

"No, now quit asking me," I told Stacey.

Boy, was I excited for our lunch break and recess. Ashley, Brooklyn, and I all sat down together to eat our lunches. Afterward, we went outside to play Volley. It's sort of like volleyball, but there's no net, and you can play with as little as two players. The game is played when someone tosses a ball up, and all players keep hitting the ball while it's in the air and never letting it hit the ground. If a player misses or drops the ball, they're out.

As the three of us were playing, Brooklyn missed her chance to hit the ball, and it rolled away from her. She chased after it but couldn't catch up to it before it rolled and hit Slime Ball Sam's foot.

"Oh sorry," Brooklyn shyly said to Sam.

"Oh look! It's Booger Face Brooklyn," Sam said as he leaned over and picked up the ball. The other boys he was playing with started to laugh.

"What? You want this?" Sam asked as he held up the red ball we were playing with.

"*Ummm,* yes. Sorry it rolled over here. Can I have it back please?" Brooklyn asked nervously.

"Well, the way I see it is, it's finders keepers. So, since I found it, I'll keep it. Now scram!" Sam yelled.

Brooklyn held her head down and turned to walk away. Just then Ashley and I walked up next to her and touched her shoulders to show her we were there for her.

"Hey, give us our ball back. She asked nicely," I said to Sam.

Sam looked at me up and down and said, "Who's going to make me?"

"Don't start with me loser. Don't forget, I remember what happened to you on the bus the first day of school. Remember Sam? Want me to tell all your friends here what happened?" I said with an attitude.

Sam's eyes got really big.

Oh, he remembered.

"You wouldn't," he said.

"Oh, but I would, so give us the ball back or I'll spill the beans," I replied.

Sam looked at me and squinted his brown eyes then looked down at the ball.

"Nobody wants this lame ball anyways," Sam said. Then he threw the ball right at my head. Luckily, I was able to catch the ball before it hit me.

"Good choice," I said with a smirk. "Come on, girls. Let's finish playing our game."

Ashley, Brooklyn, and I skipped away smiling.

"What was that all about?" Ashley asked as we stopped skipping and took a seat on the ground near the soccer field.

I told the girls, "Well, I never told anyone, but on the first day of school, Slime Ball Sam was so nervous about the third grade that he wet his pants on the bus."

Both girls then gasped.

I continued, "I gave him my sweater to wrap around his waist, and when we got into the school, I walked in front of him so no one saw his wet pants. I walked with him all the way to the nurse's office."

"Then what happened?" Ashley asked.

"I think they ended up calling his mom to bring him a new pair of pants because by recess, he was outside playing like nothing ever happened. You know he still hasn't told me thank you or returned my sweater."

Both Ashley and Brooklyn looked at me with their mouths hanging open and eyebrows raised.

"Wow, that's crazy," Ashley finally said. "But hey, accidents do happen. It does suck that he never said thank you."

"Yeah, that's messed up," Brooklyn said. "Speaking of thank you, I want to thank you both for standing up for me and having my back. You really are fantastic friends."

"That's what friends are for," Ashley said.

"Yeah, we'll always have your back. Group hug?" I replied.

The three of us leaned in and said together, "Group hug."

Chapter 8

Friday, Pie Day

Yesterday was Thankful Thursday at school. Thankful Thursdays are special because it's a day to take time out of everyone's week to highlight positive moments or people. So, yesterday I gave Brooklyn and Ashley each a picture that I drew of all three of us holding hands in a field of flowers with the words *Best Friends Forever* written across the top. I also wrote a note on the back that read:

Thank you for being my BFF.

You are always kind, funny, and fun!

Best Friends Forever and Ever!!

I gave them the drawings once we got to class in the morning. Both immediately smiled and gave me a hug.

Ashley brought cookies to share with the whole class for Thankful Thursday. Brooklyn gave Ashley and me lollipops with a note that read, *Thanks for being sweet!*

Thankful Thursdays are awesome. But nothing beats Friday, especially the last Friday of the month. At my school, every last Friday of the month is Pie Day. What is that? I am so glad you asked.

All month long the students at my school get to vote for which teachers in each grade will get a pie smashed in their face. The student with the most reading hours for their grade is the lucky one who gets to smash the pies in the teacher's face.

This month, I read a lot! I read during quiet time at school. I even read for at least thirty minutes every day at home. During today's assembly, our principal read off all the names of the students with the most reading hours for the month.

"For kindergarten, Sally St. Patrick with seventeen hours. For first grade, Kyle Phillips with twenty-one hours.

For second grade, Millie Johnson with twenty-six hours. For third grade…"

"Please, please, please, call my name," I whispered to myself. "I really want the chance to go up on the stage and smash a pie in Ms. Wiley's face."

"A.J. Waldren with…wowzers, forty-one hours of reading this month."

"Yes! Woo-hoo!" I threw both of my fists up in the air with excitement.

"For fourth grade, Tyler Smith with forty-nine hours. And finally, for fifth grade, Jasmine Jackson with fifty-five hours. Congratulations to all the top readers for the month. Keep up the good work everybody," Ms. Harrod, our principal, said with excitement.

One by one, each teacher went on to the stage and was wrapped with an art smock to cover their clothes and given clear goggles to wear to cover their eyes. Each student whose name was called got to go on stage and grab a whipped cream pie and smash it in a teacher's face. It was so awesome. All the kids at the assembly laughed and cheered. I got Ms. Wiley really good too. I even got whipped cream all in her hair. She couldn't help but to laugh.

On the bus ride home from school, the Friday Pie Day assembly was all that everyone talked about.

"You're so lucky A.J. How did it feel smashing that pie in Ms. Wiley's face?" Ashley asked.

I tried to play it cool, but I couldn't hide my excitement. "It was so fun. Like, how often does a kid get to smash a pie in their teacher's face?"

"Maybe we can do that at my birthday party tomorrow," Brooklyn said.

"Girl! Don't you know my mom would go crazy if I got whipped cream in my hair. So, *ummm,* that's a no for me," I said with a little chuckle.

"Oh, okay. Well, I have some other games we can play. Musical chairs, sack race, and limbo," Brooklyn replied.

"Sounds fun to me," Ashley said.

"Awesome. I love musical chairs," I added.

"Great. I can't wait until tomorrow. I just know it'll be the best birthday party ever," Brooklyn said with joy.

Who would have ever thought that I, A.J., would actually be looking forward to going over to Brooklyn's house for a birthday party? This weekend was going to be so much fun.

Chapter 9

FAMILY TIME

Oh, how I love Saturday mornings. My dad normally fixes breakfast for the family on these days. Sure enough, I woke up to the smell of bacon and smoked sausage cooking. I hopped out of my bed, hurried to wash my face, and brushed my teeth. I grabbed my robe, and house slippers, and made my way downstairs.

"Good morning kiddo," my dad said as he cracked an egg into a bowl.

"Morning," I replied. "Smells good." I took a seat at the kitchen counter to watch my dad.

"Thanks," he said with a smile.

"Hey guys. Good morning," my mom said as she walked into the kitchen and headed toward the refrigerator. She opened the refrigerator door and grabbed a bag of oranges.

"Good morning," my dad and I both said in unison.

"Are you making fresh-squeezed orange juice, mama?" I asked.

"Yep. Sure am. Hun, can you take the juicer down from the top cabinet for me please?" my mom asked my dad.

"A.J., help me peel these oranges please," Mom said as she looked over to me.

"Okay," I replied. "Too bad we don't have any pine-apples to go into the juicer too. That would be so good."

"Yeah, too bad. Fresh pineapples and oranges make delicious juice," Dad said.

Dad finished cracking all the eggs he was going to use to cook the scrambled eggs. He then added some shred-ded cheddar cheese to the bowl. Next, he started cooking the pancakes. He had already mixed the batter up before I came downstairs. It didn't take too long for him to cook all the pancakes.

My mom and I finished peeling the oranges and made fresh juice just as my dad was finishing up the pancakes.

"Hey A.J., go tell your sisters breakfast is ready. I'll be done cooking the scrambled eggs in a hot second," Dad said.

I ran upstairs and banged on Kayla's then Ava's door.

"Time to eat losers. Breakfast is ready!" I yelled as I ran back down the hallway and then down the stairs.

When I got downstairs and back into the kitchen, I saw my mom setting plates on the table.

"Grab the juice glasses from the counter and set them on the table, please A.J.," my mom said.

Just then, Kayla and Ava walked into the kitchen. Ava yawned and stretched her arms up into the air and said, "Morning y'all."

"Ewww! Did you brush your teeth, Ava?" I asked as I curled my upper lip and wrinkled my nose.

"Yeah, I did," Ava responded through clinched teeth.

"I'm with A.J. on this one. Ava, I can smell your breath from behind your back," Kayla said with a disgusted look.

"Well, I can smell your stinky feet through your shoes big foot!" Ava snapped back at Kayla.

"Hey, hey, hey! Settle down!" Dad blurted.

"Ava, grab the silverware and put them on the table. Kayla, grab the bacon and smoked sausage and put them on the table. A.J., get the syrup out for the pancakes," Mom ordered.

"Yeah, because the eggs are done. Let's get this breakfast party started," Dad happily said.

We all finished setting the table and placing all the food and juice on the table. We then said our grace and thanked God for the wonderful breakfast in front of us. As my mom passed me the plate with the bacon on it, she smiled at me, and I smiled back.

It was at this moment I thought, "This is my family, and as crazy as everyone is, I love them."

Chapter 10
Party Time

Brooklyn's birthday party was scheduled to start at 2 p.m., but Mom and I got to Brooklyn's house at 2:05. Ashley showed up to Brooklyn's house just as I was walking up to the front door, so I stopped and waited for her.

"Hey A.J.," Ashley said as she skipped toward me, waving hello.

"Hey Ashley," I replied. "Whatcha end up getting Brooklyn as a birthday gift?"

"I got her a Kidz Bop Karaoke microphone, a gift card to the craft store, and a pink t-shirt that says *Super Girl* on it written in blue. What about you?" Ashley said with excitement.

"I also picked out a t-shirt for her. It's purple and has the words *Good Vibes Only* written in light blue. Also, I got her a glittery orange journal to write in, and some new outfits for her Barbies."

"Nice," Ashley said.

Just as both of our moms were walking up the sidewalk toward us, Brooklyn's front door opened.

"A.J.! Ashley! You're here!" Brooklyn screamed with delight while lunging at us and hugging both of us around our shoulders. She let us go and leaned back. Her eyes were wide and filled with excitement.

"Are those for me?" Brooklyn asked as she pointed to the pink-and-white polka dotted gift bag I was holding and the teal-and-gold purse-shaped gift bag Ashley was holding.

"Happy Birthday!" Ashley and I said together as we handed Brooklyn the gift bags. Brooklyn shrieked with joy and grabbed both bags with a smile.

"Brooklyn honey, don't have everyone just standing outside. Invite them in sweetheart," Brooklyn's mom said.

"Come on. Follow me," Brooklyn said and then rushed past her mom who was standing in the doorway. Ashley and I both said hello to Brooklyn's mom and then hurried to catch up to Brooklyn.

All three of our moms chatted for a few moments, and then my mom and Ashley's mom left but planned to pick us up when the party was over.

Brooklyn led us to her backyard, which had blue and purple balloons everywhere. Balloons were tied to all the tables and lawn chairs and to each of the six chairs that were set around a large rectangle shaped table.

The table had a light purple tablecloth hanging across it. There was shiny gold, blue, and purple confetti sprinkled all over top of the table too.

Directly behind that table was the food and drinks table. Brooklyn's mom made Blue Kool-Aid and poured some into tall clear plastic cups that looked like the glasses you have when you're doing a New Year's Eve toast.

There was a large purple basket full of potato chips. There was also a fruit tray with diced pineapples, green grapes, sliced strawberries, and even orange wedges. Everything looked so fresh and juicy.

Off to the left of the food table was the dessert table. There were rows and rows of all kinds of cookies—Oreo, peanut butter, snickerdoodle, chocolate chip, sugar, and even gingerbread.

I saw empty treat bags next to the cookies, and I thought, "Don't leave this party without filling a bag with some cookies to take home."

Also on the dessert table were three large clear bowls each filled with candy. One bowl was full of miniature

Reese's cups. The next bowl was full of Jolly Ranchers. The last bowl was full of purple and blue M&M's. My second thought was, *"Fill another treat bag with scoops of candy."*

Right in the center of the dessert table was Brooklyn's blue birthday cake. It looked like someone used frosting to paint the cake to look like an ocean. It was so pretty. There were several different colors of blue swirled all over the cake. In the center of the cake, written with white frosting, were the words, *Happy 9th Birthday Brooklyn!*

"Your backyard looks so pretty Brooklyn," Ashley said.

"Thanks. I helped my mom hang the purple and blue streamers up all around the fence. I hope you like Blue Raspberry and Lemonade Kool-Aid."

Ashley and I looked at each other, smiled, and then looked back to Brooklyn and said, "We love it."

"Hey Brooklyn, look who's here," Brooklyn's mom said. Brooklyn turned around and screamed, "Emma!" Both girls ran toward one another and then hugged.

"Hey guys, this is my cousin Emma. She's nine years old too. Her birthday was two weeks ago."

We all said hi to each other and smiled.

"Let's get this party started by playing a game of musical chairs," Brooklyn's dad said as he walked out into the backyard holding a large speaker in one hand and an iPad in the other. Brooklyn's two younger brothers were following right behind him.

All of us kids jumped up and down and screamed with excitement. Brooklyn's parents grabbed all the chairs from around the table and lined them up three in a row and back-to-back. Brooklyn's dad started to play Kidz Bop songs.

During the first round of musical chairs, all the kids had a chair to sit in. During the next round, Brooklyn's mom took away one of the chairs. That meant there were six kids trying to sit down in five chairs.

Sure enough, when the music stopped, Brooklyn's baby brother was left standing without a chair to sit in. As a two-year-old I don't think he understood how to play the game. He started crying. Brooklyn's mom scooped him up and took him inside the house.

"Let's keep going. I'll take this chair away now," Brooklyn's dad said.

Then there were five kids and only four chairs. Brooklyn's dad turned the music back on, and all the kids start marching around the four chairs. The next kid to get out the game was Brooklyn's five-year-old brother. At least he didn't cry. He just stood next to his dad and helped start and stop the music on the iPad.

After a few intense minutes of playing, the last two kids left marching around the one chair was Brooklyn and Emma. They were staring each other in the eyes. Their faces were so tight that you knew they meant business.

The music was playing loudly through the speakers. Emma and Brooklyn were circling the chair with so much concentration.

"Oh my gosh, my armpits are sweating," Ashley said as we all looked on with anticipation.

And then the music stopped. It seemed like everything was moving in slow motion. Brooklyn's eyes widened as she lunged for the chair. Emma's mouth opened wide, and you could hear her yell out, "Nooooo!" as she reached for the chair.

Emma was just half a second too slow. Brooklyn sat down in the chair first nearly knocking it over. Everyone jumped up and yelled, "Ooooh!"

"That was a close one!" I shouted.

"Wow. Good game girls. You really know how to keep us all in suspense," Brooklyn's dad said.

"I want a rematch," Emma said. "I was so close to winning the game."

All the kids decided we all wanted a rematch, so we grabbed chairs and set them up again. This round, Ashley won in the showdown against Brooklyn.

After two games of musical chairs, Brooklyn's mom finally came back out of the house with Brooklyn's little brother who was eating a Popsicle.

"Who's ready for a sack race?" she asked.

Every kid jumped up and down while raising their hands and screaming, "Me! Me! Me!"

"Awesome! Here, each of you grab a laundry bag as your sack," Brooklyn's mom said, pointing to a box near the fence. All five kids grabbed a sack. Brooklyn's baby brother just sat at the table eating his Popsicle.

"Line up at this side of the yard as the starting point," Brooklyn's dad directed us. Then he said, "Okay, now everyone needs to step inside their sack. When you hear my whistle blow, everyone start hopping. The first person to make it to the finish line at the opposite side of the yard wins."

"I know I'm going to beat you all. I've been practicing all week long," Brooklyn's five-year-old brother said.

"We'll just see about that," Brooklyn said with an evil grin.

"On your marks. Get set." Brooklyn's dad looked us all in the eyes. I took a long deep breath and exhaled.

The whistle blew, and we all took off hopping. Ashley was the first to go down. She got a good four or five hops in and crashed to the ground laughing.

Emma was next to go down. Brooklyn was in the lead with her brother and me hopping close behind. I felt like I was hopping to save my life.

Brooklyn just so happened to trip up and fall. I thought, "*Yes! This is my chance to take the lead.*" Everyone started chanting, "Go! Go! Go!"

Brooklyn's little brother was still in the race. His five-year-old legs were still hopping. He was not letting up. I saw nothing but determination in his eyes. And that is when it happened. I tripped and fell.

With two more hops, Brooklyn's brother made it all the way to the finish line. He threw his hands into the air and yelled, "Who's the man?"

If I had only concentrated on myself and what I was doing instead of looking at others, I could have won.

"Good job. Way to stay focused," I said to Brooklyn's little brother as I walked over to give him a high five. Everyone clapped and congratulated him with a pat on the back and a high five.

"Alright, limbo time!" Brooklyn shouted.

Brooklyn's dad grabbed what looked like a broomstick and repeated, "Limbo time."

Both of Brooklyn's parents grabbed one end of the broomstick, and all the kids got in a line. The sounds of Caribbean Island music played from the speakers. Everyone started singing, "How low can you go? Yeah! How low can you go?"

One by one, all the kids leaned backward slightly and walked underneath the broomstick. Brooklyn's parents steadily lowered the broomstick after everyone got a turn. It finally got to a point where the broomstick was let down to about as low as our waists. Emma fell first, then Ashley, followed by me. Brooklyn and her brother took their turns and went underneath the broomstick.

"Wowzers. You two are good," I said.

Brooklyn's parents lowered the broomstick even lower. Down went Brooklyn first and then down went her brother. Both started laughing uncontrollably.

"It's a tie!" Brooklyn's dad yelled.

Everyone clapped and cheered. Brooklyn's dad then received an alert on his cellphone. "Right on time. The pizza delivery just arrived," Brooklyn's dad said and headed towards the front door.

"Great job everyone. Now, I am sure you've all worked up an appetite, so run inside, wash your hands, and let's eat some cheese pizza." Brooklyn's mom said.

"Yeah!" all the kids screamed.

After we all washed our hands, we sat around the decorated table. Brooklyn's parents served us the pizza. Ashley and Emma both asked for some chips.

"May I have some grapes and orange slices too please?" I asked.

"Yeah, me too please," Brooklyn said.

"Yes, you girls may have some fruit," Brooklyn's mom responded. Then Brooklyn's mom placed a cup of blue Kool-Aid in front of each kid.

"This party is so awesome Brooklyn," Ashley said.

"Yeah, I'm having so much fun. Thanks again for inviting me," I said.

After we ate, we all were able to get a few treat bags and fill them with cookies and candy.

"I'm going to have to hide these cookies from my mom. Talk about a real live cookie monster. That woman loves her some cookies," I said as I put two snickerdoodle cookies into my treat bag.

"Don't hide the cookies A.J. Just make your mom her own cookie goodie bag," Brooklyn's mom said.

"Good idea," I replied.

"Can I open up my presents now?" Brooklyn asked.

"Sure thing, Hun," Brooklyn's mom responded.

Everyone gathered around Brooklyn as she sat in her chair. Brooklyn's dad passed her each gift, one at a time.

"*Ooooh. Aww.* That's cute!" is all you heard each time Brooklyn opened a gift. Once all the gifts were opened and Brooklyn gave everyone a hug, she threw up her hands and yelled, "cake time!" with a smile.

Brooklyn's dad grabbed the blue cake from the dessert table and placed it in front of Brooklyn. Her mom put nine candles on top of the cake and then lit them with a match.

"Okay. Let's all sing. And a one, and a two, and a three. Altogether," Brooklyn's mom said.

We all began to sing, "Happy Birthday," to Brooklyn. Brooklyn's face was filled with so much joy. Her eyes shined and her smile was so big that it literally stretched across her entire face and every tooth in her mouth was showing.

When we all finished singing, Brooklyn's mom leaned over her, grabbed her shoulders from behind, and said, "make a wish sweetheart."

Brooklyn took a deep breath, paused, and closed her eyes. Then she blew out all nine candles with one try.

Everyone erupted into a cheer and started clapping. Brooklyn looked around at everyone, still smiling.

The birthday party was finally wrapping up. Emma was the first person to be picked up. All of us girls agreed we needed to set up a playdate so we could all hang out again.

Ashley's mom was the next to arrive.

"Thanks again for an awesome time Brooklyn," Ashley said as she gave Brooklyn a hug, then she skipped down the walkway and climbed into her mom's car, waving as they drove away.

Brooklyn and I were sitting in the chairs on her front porch waiting for my mom to pick me up.

"What was your favorite part of today?" Brooklyn asked me.

"Musical chairs and the sack race," I replied with a smile. "Emma's face was sooo funny as she reached for the chair during musical chairs. It's like she couldn't believe she wasn't going to sit down first and beat you. She was just so shocked, and seeing her reaching out and yelling, nooooo! Oh my gosh, that was so funny!" I said.

Then Brooklyn and I started laughing again.

"How about yours?" I asked Brooklyn.

Brooklyn looked up and out into the distant sky. She started to smile and tucked her hair behind her ears and then looked at me and said, "Everything. Today was the best day of my entire life. I have never had so much fun and laughed so much. Thank you for coming to my birthday party."

"*Awww.* I wouldn't have missed it for nothing. BFF's forever," I said.

"BFFs forever," Brooklyn agreeingly said.

Just then my mom's car pulled up to the curb in front of Brooklyn's house.

"Thanks again. See ya later," I said.

Brooklyn and I hugged, but she didn't let me go right away. We stood and hugged for a few extra seconds.

As we were hugging, she whispered to me, "I believe my wish is already coming true thanks to you. Having a real friend who truly cares about me is all I ever wanted."

My name is Aleah Jean, except, mostly everyone calls me A.J., but the truth is my favorite thing to be called is a true friend.

About the Author

Kimberly Waldren was born on a military base in Naples, Italy in 1982. Growing up a military brat, Kimberly was afforded the grand opportunity to travel all around the world. This created many fun-filled experiences and adventures as a child. With those memories, Kimberly decided to happily share some of her childhood stories with the world through AJ. AJ and the Annoying Copy-Catter is Kimberly's first children's book. If she isn't spending time with her husband and two daughters traveling, you can almost always find her in the kitchen cooking or baking.

Made in United States
Orlando, FL
07 December 2022